Cross
Katie Kross

Donna Morrissey

Illustrated by
Bridgette Morrissey

PUFFIN
an imprint of Penguin Canada

Published by the Penguin Group
Penguin Group (Canada), 90 Eglinton Avenue East, Suite 700, Toronto, Ontario, Canada
M4P 2Y3 (a division of Pearson Canada Inc.)

Penguin Group (USA) Inc., 375 Hudson Street, New York, New York 10014, U.S.A.
Penguin Books Ltd, 80 Strand, London WC2R 0RL, England
Penguin Ireland, 25 St Stephen's Green, Dublin 2, Ireland (a division of Penguin Books Ltd)
Penguin Group (Australia), 250 Camberwell Road, Camberwell, Victoria 3124, Australia
(a division of Pearson Australia Group Pty Ltd)
Penguin Books India Pvt Ltd, 11 Community Centre, Panchsheel Park, New Delhi – 110 017, India
Penguin Group (NZ), 67 Apollo Drive, Rosedale, Auckland 0632, New Zealand
(a division of Pearson New Zealand Ltd)
Penguin Books (South Africa) (Pty) Ltd, 24 Sturdee Avenue, Rosebank, Johannesburg 2196, South Africa

Penguin Books Ltd, Registered Offices: 80 Strand, London WC2R 0RL, England

First published 2012

1 2 3 4 5 6 7 8 9 10 (FR)

Copyright © Donna Morrissey, 2012
Illustrations copyright © Bridgette Morrissey, 2012

Bridgette extends a deep thank you to the Nova Scotia Department of Communities, Culture and
Heritage for its support in the illustration of this book.

Manufactured in Canada.

LIBRARY AND ARCHIVES CANADA CATALOGUING IN PUBLICATION

Morrissey, Donna, 1956-

Cross Katie Kross / Donna Morrissey ; illustrated by Bridgette Morrissey.

ISBN 978-0-670-06479-3

I. Morrissey, Bridgette II. Title.

PS8576.O74164C76 2012   jC813'.54   C2011-906596-7

Visit the Penguin Canada website at **www.penguin.ca**

Special and corporate bulk purchase rates available;
please see **www.penguin.ca/corporatesales** or call 1-800-810-3104, ext. 2477.

For **Bentley**,
we love you.

Old Katie Kross was having a wonderful dream.
It was about a place called Love Valley, where the grass
was as soft as ducks' feathers and the air smelled sweet
with flowers and the sun shimmered gold on a pond.
Rabbits played peekaboo amongst the bushes, and
yellow warblers sang to Katie from the trees, and squirrels
dropped chestnuts onto her lap, and Old Katie Kross
scampered with them around the meadow, waving
as they scooted to the treetops.

It was a beautiful dream, and
Old Katie Kross was very happy.

KERRR-KERRR-KERRROOO!!!

Katie Kross startled awake.

"Jumpins! Morning again," she grumbled, and pulled the pillow over her ears as the rooster kept

KERR-KERR-KERROOING

and the hens

CLUCK-CLUCK-CLUCKED

around her front step, wanting to be fed.

Jumpins. Katie Kross didn't like mornings. She didn't like feeding the rooster and chickens. She didn't like the shrieking children playing near her front step. Sometimes she chased them away with her broom. She didn't like washing her face either, or weeding her garden, or going to market.

She tried to go back to sleep, but the milkman knocked on her door. She didn't like the milkman. She didn't like broccoli and carrots and tomatoes and all the other yucky food that grew in her garden or that her neighbours gave her.

Katie Kross liked ice cream. She liked candies and cakes and puddings. She got tummy aches a lot, and the doctor told her she ate too many sweets. She didn't like the doctor.

"I don't like most anything!" Katie yelled as she got out of bed. "I don't like this house, and I don't like gardens or neighbours or shrieking children.

Oh, I wish I lived in Love Valley!"

She opened her eyes wide. "Why, of course!" she said. "That's it! I'll go and live in Love Valley. It shouldn't be hard to find, for I've already seen it in my dream."

So Katie Kross packed some puddings and cakes, and then she set off down her pathway and onto a dusty road. She walked toward the sun.

She walked and walked. She walked for many days. Then, much to her dismay, the road arrived at a crossroads where it split off in three different directions. "Which way shall I go?" Katie Kross asked herself.

At that moment a mean-looking rabbit hopped out of the forest. He stood with his paws on his haunches, and his nose twitched rapidly as he stared at Katie.

"Can you tell me which road leads to Love Valley?" Katie asked him, a little timidly, for he looked very unfriendly.

"This one, naturally," said the rabbit, jabbing at the first road with a big clawy paw. "Can't you see how straight it is and how easy it is to walk on? And how well-trodden it is? Everybody follows this road. Obviously, this road leads to Love Valley."

"Why, of course!" said Katie. "*Of course*, I should've seen that."

"Follow me!" ordered the rabbit. "But stay behind me!"
Katie looked at the big bully rabbit. She looked down the well-trodden road.
The rabbit's tail twitched impatiently.

"I'm coming, I'm coming … jumpins!" said Katie Kross,
and she followed the rabbit.

She followed him a long way. She followed him past cornfields and potato fields and hayfields and fields that grew nothing at all. She followed him across bridges and railway tracks. She followed and followed. Her feet began to hurt, and her eyes itched from the dust.

Soon, the road ended,

and the rabbit vanished into the woods.

Katie stared at the woods. "Jumpins, what's this? Where's Love Valley?" she cried. "How can a road end before it gets somewhere?"

She looked around for the rabbit. "You silly old bunny!" she yelled. "I walked all this way. It's all your fault!" She stomped angrily around a little bush, shouting,

"I'll never trust rabbits again!

I'll never trust rabbits again!"

Katie started back the way she had come. She was very cross.
She walked back up the road all day. Dust made her eyes itch and
itch. Her shoes hurt her feet. Her legs grew very, very tired.
She slept beside a brook that kept her awake with its babbling.

"Jumpins," she muttered. "Why do brooks babble so loudly?"

She got up and started walking again. Finally, she was back at the crossroads where the road split in three.

She looked down the middle road. "Oh my goodness!" she exclaimed. The road was smoothly paved and shiny, with bright-coloured street lights and richly built houses and trees all decorated with scrumptious-looking fruit and bushes that grew cute little nibblies that smelled like chocolate.

A fox strolled out of the woods, his fluffy red tail held high and proud and sparkling with sequins.

"Oh, Fox," she called, "is this the road to Love Valley?"

The fox proudly swished his tail. "But of course," he said. "This is the most exciting of all roads. I"—and he swished his lovely red tail again—"am well known here. Everyone just loves my thick, fluffy coat and its richly red colour."

He yawned. "Mmm, if you'll excuse me, I must nap before my evening's festivities." He picked a nibbly from a nearby bush and popped it in his mouth, then disappeared down a rose-edged burrow.

"Why, of course," said Katie Kross.
"Of course the road to Love Valley would be shiny with riches and comforts. Jumpins, why didn't I think of that? Oh, foxes are much more clever than rabbits."

So Katie set off down the shiny paved road. She walked and walked.
She bit into a cute little chocolate-smelling nibbly—and her mouth soured!
She spat it out. "Jumpins, tastes like coffee!" she cried.
"How can chocolate
taste like coffee?"

She kept walking. The hard pavement started hurting her feet. It wore holes through her shoes. The bright-coloured lights hurt her eyes. They shone all night long and wouldn't let her sleep. Dark circles lined her eyes and her hair grew limp and her dress tattered around her legs. Children ran away from her because she looked like a witch.

Katie walked and walked. And then the road ended!

"What, again?" Katie Kross jumped up and down. "Jumpins!" she screamed. "Another road that leads nowhere? I won't have it, I won't have it! I want to go to Love Valley!"

She jumped up and down in such a rage that the birds fell silent in the forest and the wind ceased to blow. She kicked at an ornamented tree till her shoe fell off.

She stormed back up the shiny paved road, fuming and hollering. She would get even with that snooty fox and with that bully rabbit, too. She would find Love Valley and she would put up a fence and nobody would get in, nobody but herself.

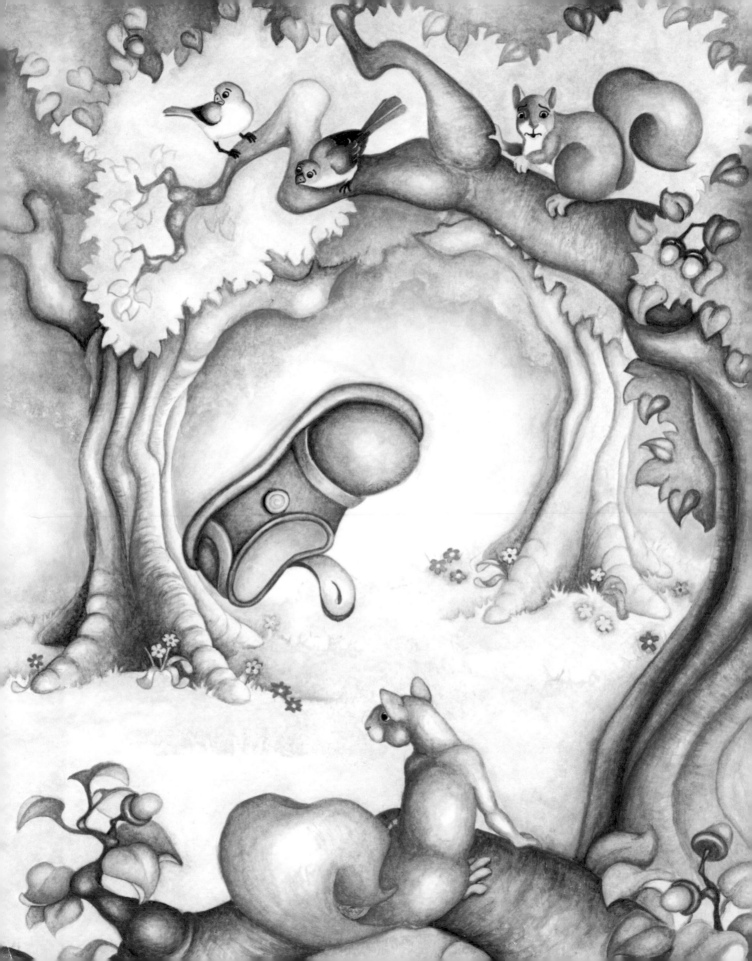

When she got back to the crossroads, she sniffed. There was only one road left. It curled through a dark, shaggy woods and was overgrown with sprawling roots and droopy, saggy flowers and fat wads of weeds.

"Of course this is the road to Love Valley," Katie said to herself. "There are no footprints and no silly animals, and I can do what I want. Oh look, what a lovely fountain."

She drank long from the pink juice bubbling out of the fountain. It tasted sweet and cool and made her stomach feel good. She walked down the road, and the grass was soft beneath her feet. She waved to the birds chirping and flitting overhead and gazed at the sun shimmering gold on the pond.

Why, it was just like the Love Valley in her dream! She was almost there, and she sang and danced and pranced merrily down the road.

Suddenly, it grew darkish. Katie tripped over
tree roots and the tangly, droopy flowers.

Like magic, another fountain appeared, and then another.
Katie drank long and deep, and the sun sparkled rainbows through the
trees, and she laughed again, and sang and danced down the road.

Katie kept drinking and dancing till the fountain juice no longer tasted sweet, but bitter, and made her tummy ache. She stopped drinking from the magic fountains. The woods became dark and stayed dark. There were so many tree roots that Katie kept tripping. She lost her shoes and scraped her knees and hurt her hands. She heard strange noises and became afraid.

"Hello?" she called out, but nobody answered. She felt frightened and alone, and her feet began to bleed. She dropped wearily to the ground.

"Jumpins," she moaned. "There is no Love Valley! I'm a fool to believe in dreams. I want to go home."

She began to cry. She cried and cried. She cried till her tears washed the dark from her eyes and she could see clearly through the forest.

Then she bandaged her feet with a piece of her dress and began the long trek back through the dark, shaggy woods.

After many days Katie Kross arrived home. The hens were roosting in her loft, but she didn't care. She hunted for nuts with the squirrels and raccoons in her garden. She ate some peas and tomatoes growing amongst the weeds in her vegetable patch, and her tummy felt good. She swept her floors and front step and went to sit beside the brook. Its babbling soothed her.

Children from the village crept through the forest to stare curiously at the old woman sleeping beside the brook. They drew back in fright when she awakened.

"Did you hurt yourself?" a boy asked her.

"Yes, I did," she said softly.

"It was right here, under my nose.

I call it Love Valley."

Katie looked at her feet. She became very still. She felt the grass as soft as ducks' feathers beneath her. She saw the squirrels scampering up the trees with chestnuts. She heard the yellow warblers chirping from the bushes and saw the sun sparkling golden on the brook. Her hands trembled, and tears trickled down her wrinkly face.

"I was walking for a long time," she said. "I was looking for a nice place to live."

"Did you find it?" asked a girl.

Katie Kross smiled. She leaned forward and tickled the girl's nose.